The Wind of
a Thousand Years

Albert's Manuscript

Patricia Jamie Lee, MA

*M*any *K*ites *P*ress

www.manykites.com

ISBN 9781937238018

Dear Reader,

For many years I was working on a novel series in which the characters continually seek the intersection between heaven and earth. In one of the novels a character named Albert showed up, an old man by then, with a mysterious manuscript that told of his journey to the spirit world as a young Lakota man. Albert's Manuscript was woven into the main novel, but I had no idea of its contents. One winter day in 2004 I felt stuck in my writing and decided to see what the manuscript actually said.

I went a bought a cheap spiral bound notebook and started writing. Albert's manuscript emerged over six days in quick nonstop writing sessions. I was simply carried into his story. I put no pressure on the words to perform, asked nothing of them, and allowed Albert's manuscript to be whatever it wanted to be. When it was done, it was done. Nothing more could be added.

Albert is not a real person, not in this realm anyway. You will not find him here, but I suspect he is not very far away—and had something he wanted to say. I was willing to listen and write.

Since that time, I created a short version of *The Wind of a Thousand Year,* illustrated it myself, and sent it out into the world with my little Bead People. Since that time, over seven thousand copies of the little *Wind* book have gone to over 40 countries carrying their message of peace. Do check out The Bead People International Peace Project to read the story and get involved. The website is www.thebeadpeople.com. Also, visit me at my blog, No Ordinary Life and join our community of peacemakers by subscribing at www.jamieleeonline.com. We certainly could use a little more peace in the world.

As for me, I'm loving my new life in northern Minnesota in our little hand-built straw bale house with our gardens expanding around us. Tell me about your life.

And now, here is Albert and Jilly's story.

Sincerely . . .

Patricia Jamie Lee

1

A Note from Jilly

Dear Friends,

Following is the story my Grandfather Albert told me over five days in the summer of 2001. His notes were a hodgepodge of pages scribbled over many years, and he needed time to organize his thoughts. When he was ready, I recorded his words as he told them and later transcribed the manuscript that appears here.

We took frequent breaks. During some of those breaks, Grandfather continued to scribble more notes that I didn't read until later. I've added those into the manuscript in italics because I didn't want to leave out the smallest flavor of his thoughts. I hope you gain as much from my grandfather's story as I have.

Sincerely,

Jilly

Day One

Morning Session

"So we begin at last, Jilly."

"Yes, Grandfather. I'm all set up. Begin whenever you're ready."

"Thank you, my dear.

When I was a young boy I used to look at my grandfather and see his bones beneath his thin skin and wonder how he crawled out of bed each day and forced those old bones to carry him around. Now, I have become him. I am old and need to tell this story before the creator takes me home.

My great-grandfather lost his wife and first child at the Wounded Knee Massacre, shot down dead in the snow. His name was Gerald and his wife's name was Tilde. They say when he heard the news of Tilde's and Sarah's deaths, he went blind in one eye—as if he couldn't stand to see but half the world after that terrible winter day. Grandfather lived to be 74. I am 72, nearly as old as he was when he died.

My hand doesn't work so well anymore, so I am telling this story to my granddaughter Jilly, a pretty 23-year-old college student home for a break. It is slow work for her, sitting nearby as I sort a blizzard of paper scraps. My memories have come to me in bits and pieces, and I have scribbled them down on whatever was handy. Such an odd collection of words on the backs of napkins and placemats or scribbled into small notebooks bought at convenience stores for a quarter. Jilly is one of the new ones, they told me, the children who would walk out of the long storm and make a new world.

She winks at me as I record these words. They are wise, these new children of earth. It is for them that I write—so they can better understand who they are and why they have come at this time. They are the seventh generation.

"Isn't that right, Jilly?"

"What, Grandfather?"

"Nothing. You look like my secretary sitting there with your little recorder."

"I just want to be sure I get it all. If I record it first and then transcribe it, I won't miss anything. I can't write as fast as you can speak. Besides," she smiled at me. "I just want to listen. Do you want another cup of coffee?"

"Please. It will give me a minute to organize my thoughts."

Outside the morning sun is bright and yellow over the land. At last I take the time to get this story down. I have carried it so long it feels like a part of my bones. I wonder, will I get light as air when it is told and drift off into the clouds? I wonder.

"Here you go, Grandfather. Go on now."

After Wounded Knee my remaining relatives stayed on Pine Ridge Reservation although Grandfather was Minneconjou. When he remarried, he married an Oglala Lakota woman named Kathryn. They had three sons and two daughters but, of the five, only one made it into adult life—my father, Joseph. There was a lot of death in those days. There still is. My mother once told me it was because the souls of the living went in search of the souls of the dead.

Joseph married Clara in 1927, and together they had eight children, but four died before the age of ten. I was one who lived, the oldest boy. I believe that what my mother said was true—about the living looking for the dead souls. I know I tried mighty hard to die.

When I was eighteen, my father was shot in the head. A hunting accident, they said—but death on Pine Ridge is never an accident. Mother said he was shot by history, that history holds a shotgun to all of our heads. I didn't know what she meant at the time, but now, as I look back, it is clear. By age twenty I had hardened into a drinking, fighting young man. I was red with rage and living in that twenty-year-old body was like living in the center of a volcano.

I lived with my mamma and two sisters in a beat up little cabin on the north edge of Pine Ridge Village. It was 1948. I would have been in the army except my father's death relieved me of duty. My duty was to my mother— not that I was much good to her. She needed me to be the man of the family, but I was a hotheaded kid and had been since my father was shot.

It was summer, near the fourth of July. There was going to be a big powwow and feast celebrating the returning vets, but my father's death had even robbed me of that honor. I wanted out of there, one way or another.

The night before the powwow two buddies and I started celebrating early with cheap whiskey, but the booze only stirred the volcano cooking in my middle. It was midmorning when I stumbled home still half-drunk and Mamma met me on the stoop. Just the sight of her standing there on that beat up porch in her bathrobe threw me over the edge. She'd been crying.

"I need you Albert," she said. "I need you to be a man now. Your father is gone, and I can't do this alone." Mamma spoke Lakota, so I grew up hearing English and Lakota mixed up in my head like word soup. She took a step toward me. "He isn't coming back, Albert."

In almost two years she'd hardly spoken of my father. Why she chose that moment to start isn't clear, but when she said I had to be the man now something in me broke loose. I held my breath trying to get my head to stop spinning. "Don't Mamma," I begged.

"Albert."

She said my name like it meant something. It didn't mean anything. I did not exist.

"He's dead, Albert. Your father is gone."

A fierce heat rose up in me, and I turned to her and said, "You think he's gone? He is not gone. He can't be. I'll get him back, Mamma. I will." I stomped past her and went into the cabin.

She followed close behind, crying aloud now and murmuring my name. I grabbed a duffle bag and started stuffing it with whatever was near—a canteen, a can of beans, some stale crackers. I was a crazy man, not even clear what I was doing. My two sisters, Shawna and Sylvie, came out of the one bedroom still in their cotton nightgowns looking sleepy and disturbed. "Go back to bed." I yelled at them.

Mamma tried to hold my arm, but I gave it a rough shake. She backed up and took a place in front of my sisters as if afraid for them. There was fear in her eyes. I hated seeing that fear more than anything.

I turned and ran out the door. I needed to get the hell out of there before I covered them all with this red rage that had taken my spirit.

Mamma followed me outside. I dropped the duffle, went to the shed, and took down the saddle. I flung it over the back of poor George, our old, sway back horse. My hands shook as I tried to buckle it. I turned to my Mamma and said, "I'll bring him back to you, Mamma. I swear."

Mamma screamed at me. "You can't, Albert. Don't you see? He's dead, and you can't reach him anymore."

"I damn well can. I'll go to the ancestors and tell them to give me back my father." I climbed on George's back and rode off. When I looked back, Mamma was curled on the ground weeping and moaning, "Oh, my boy, my son, don't go. Please don't go."

I had only one goal as I charged off. I was going to bring my father back—or die trying. It was July—the sun at midmorning was already scorching, riding above me on its own race to hell. Within minutes I was sweating, my horse was sweating, the whole damn world was sweating. I wanted a cold beer—but in my twisted mind I thought the ancestors wouldn't like it if I showed up with beer on my breath.

Looking back now, I'd gone plumb crazy. My mind flickered with ugly images, all that I'd seen and done, all that had been done to us. It felt like history was a dark tunnel, and I was riding through that black tunnel, time flying by me. The images killed me again and again. I saw death, so much death. My younger brothers broken to bits in a car wreck, my dad with his brains splashed over the prairie, my uncle hanging by his neck in a shed, that same shed burning one night when I couldn't stand to look at it any longer. Suddenly, I felt like it was raining down blood on me, a steady torrent of blood. It was getting in my eyes, blurring my vision, smelling of iron and rust and death. One eye went blind like my grandfather's and then the other eye went blind, and I then I saw nothing but blackness. It scared the hell out of me. I hung on to the reins, clutching the leather as I raced forward in the dark, dark world.

Old George must have sensed he had a blind, crazy man on his back. He slowed his pace, went to a trot and then, as if that horse knew what was about to happen, he sought the only shade for miles and miles. He clopped over to a small grove of trees and stopped. I slid out of the saddle and collapsed to the ground and passed out. Later, I figured out that I lay passed out beneath that grove for almost two full days.

That was the beginning. I have spent the fifty plus years since putting together all that I learned while unconscious those two days. I suspect, on reading similar reports from other people that I died but was led back to life by those same ancestors I sought in such a mad frenzy. I was led back so I could tell this story to the best of my ability. They made me a Watcher during that time. And in seventy-two years, I've only met a few other Watchers.

The place my spirit woke up to while my blind and broken body lay beneath the grove of trees was not a place I had ever even imagined. I don't know if *place* is the right word to describe it, more like presence. In this presence, all around me was clearly created as energy and not form. The images and structures were shifting and changing like the northern lights. It was like standing inside of Aurora Borealis, but with the light able to fashion and refashion itself within seconds. In a moment, cities, landscapes, whole worlds formed and dissolved again only to be replaced by other cities and worlds. The changing scenes fascinated me—like the first time I ever saw a motion picture when I was a boy. I checked out my hands, my legs, my trunk and all seemed there, yet I was aware of them more as points of being rather than a whole, solid body.

My first focused thought was that I had finally done it. I had made it into the realm of the ancestors. And the second thought was that I must be dead. I felt sad and ashamed. I'd left my mother and sisters when they most needed me. With this shame a curtain dropped and all the wonderful, changing city-worlds blinked out like a candle and now I was surrounded in gray, like a fog, only more dense and dreary than any fog I'd known in life. It was a dim, cheerless place, and I thought that the priests and nuns had lied. Hell was not fire and brimstone but this—a gray, dim curtain of gray, the absence of light.

Then, through the gray and the fog and the mist, a single figure emerged and came to stand beside me. The sight stunned me. I saw that the man carried all the beautiful cities with him. It was my Great Grandfather.

"Jilly, honey, can we take a short break? Have a cup of coffee maybe?"

13

Albert's Notes

With a nod Jilly excuses herself and goes into the kitchen. I hear the gas flame pop beneath the coffee pot, a cupboard door open and close as she brews us a pot of coffee. I need a moment to collect myself. Even though her little machine continues to record, I write these words while she is gone.

Oh, to recall what it was to see my grandfather again. Although he was my great grandfather, I just think of him as grandfather. In truth, the image of my grandfather overwhelmed me then and overwhelms me now these many decades later. I'd thought him lost to me forever, but there he was, standing in front of me with cities flickering in his hand, and the truth in his eyes. I realized that if I could see him again, then all others I thought lost to me in death were nearby as well. Unless, of course, I had joined them in that place of death.

Jilly returns with my coffee. I take the hot cup and palm it in both hands. Now to proceed with my story, to record the events of that unusual two-day journey, a journey that guided the rest of my days, including this one in which I sit now.

"Thank you Jilly. Are you ready?"

"Yes, Grandfather."

As soon as my grandfather came near me the gray net lifted. I was once again in a flashing, brilliant world of shifting cities and mountain ranges and vivid blue seas. Grandfather wrapped his arms around me and kissed my cheeks. "It's good to see you, grandson."

He stared into my eyes, and I saw that his blindness was gone. So was mine. I had nearly forgotten the bloody, blinding rain. "Grandfather, what has happened? Where are we? Have I died then?" The gray curtain began to drop like a heavy fishing net as I thought again of my mamma and my sisters. Grandfather flicked his hand quick as though swatting a fly and the gray net flew off again.

"No, Grandson, you are not dead, only here for a very short while. There is much I need to tell you and not much time. If you stay too long you will not find your way back. Come now, we must hurry."

Grandfather turned and began walking quickly. I grew dizzy and nearly passed out again. When my vision cleared, a woman stood beside him. She said, "Gerald, give the poor boy a moment to find his feet. Can't you see he is confused?"

Like Grandfather, she'd just appeared from nowhere. I stared at her. I knew I'd never seen her before, and yet felt I knew her. She was so beautiful, a long braid swinging down her back like a thick dark vine, and when she spied me gaping at her, she chuckled. "I'm Tilde. Unci to you." *Unci* means Grandmother in Lakota.

15

My jaw must have dropped. Grandfather laughed and said, "Albert, this is Tilde, my first wife. Ain't she a beauty?"

I understood suddenly why my grandfather would shutter one eye when such a pretty wife died in the snow. But they were not dead, not blind, not bleeding on a frosty ground in Pine Ridge. They looked more alive than all the folks I knew who were still wandering their days in life.

Unci palmed my face as if I were three. I felt three. "I know I'm not your blood grandmother—Kathryn was—but what she lost, I gained, and so we are connected. What a precious boy. What an unhappy boy. Come on, your grandfather has much to explain."

Then to my shock, Grandfather reached over and grabbed Tilde like a lusty young man and kissed her silver. It was odd, that these particle bodies could rearrange themselves in a split second. Suddenly Grandfather was a young man with his bride and, when he kissed her again, golden glitter flew off Tilde's body like lust dust.

I started laughing so hard I had to hold my sides and glitter flew from my body too. My mind was spinning. I figured I really had gone crazy on that old horse with that big anger riding my back and never would find the real world again. I squeezed my eyes shut, and when I opened them again, Grandfather was an old man again and Unci

16

had shed her glittering youth and grown old with him. She was still beautiful. "Jesus man," I muttered. "Where the hell am I?"

Unci shook her head and grinned. "Watch your mouth, boy. Show some respect for the dead."

Grandfather caught the glint of laughter in her eyes and chuckled. "Hush, Tilde. He doesn't understand any of this." To me he said, "Nothing is solid, son. That is the first lesson I am to give you. There is only the appearance of a solid world."

He talked in riddles. I was confused clear down to my toes, and when I looked down at my own body, it was no longer that of a young man but a boy, maybe seven-years-old. I remembered the way he'd carved a small whistle for me out of a reed and taught me to play it. The whistle was long gone, but I could still hear the hollow, whispery sound of it—like wind whistling through trees. My throat thickened, and I felt like bawling.

Grandfather watched me. "See, son. It is all a whisper, like the sound of that whistle. Here for a moment, then changed. Come on. We best get started." And he took Tilde's hand and they walked toward a shimmering range of mountains. As they stepped on this shifting land, a path of blue appeared before them. It looked as if it were made of satin or water. I couldn't be sure. I followed them.

"Ah, Jilly, I always wanted to paint that path. I tried to learn to paint just to see if I could lay down an image of that place, but I was bad at it, worse than bad, actually. Maybe your artist friend, what is her name? June? Maybe she could grab those pictures out of my head and paint them."

"I think she could, Grandpa. I really think she could paint them." Jilly dropped her head, and I saw tears flowing down her face.

"What is it, my girl? Why are you crying?"

"Its June, Grandfather. I just found out she may be dying. She has cancer and is at the Mayo for treatment, but they say the cancer is running through her like a fire." A sob caught in her throat. "I may never see her again."

"Shut your little machine off, dear. That is enough for now. Why don't you take that old dog for a quick run?"

Albert's Notes

When Jilly cried, I put my hand on her head, but said nothing. Even with it all, I could not offer comfort to those who felt that gray net. I never could. There was no removing it with words. Each person had to find their own flick of a hand, their own understanding of why death, why loss. How do you tell these hearts that love so deeply that feel so deeply, that nothing is lost? It's like my desire to paint the images—they cannot be captured, not with color, not with words, only with the spirit. All I can do is tell this story to the best of my ability and let people do with it what they will.

I leaned over and kissed the top of Jilly's head and told her, "June will see those images, my dear. And when she sees that shimmering land, brushes will appear like magic in her hand and she will paint, and paint, and paint." I tell her we are through for now and send her off into the bright sunshine to walk Hound Dog. He's not really a hound dog, but he likes the name. He's really a mutt that showed up here two years ago to share my old age and keep me company.

Out the front window I watch Jilly and Hound Dog run down the drive. She tosses the gray net into the winds, up to the sunshine, down to the earth to take her sorrow away—another indicator that she is one of them. She understands from which direction true healing comes—from the earth, only from the earth.

Jilly is spending a week with me to help me sort my notes and get what I can on paper. She is twenty-three and the world swirls around her like a circus. It is summer outside my door and autumn inside my soul. The prairie outside my window is golden, my favorite color in all of creation. It is the only gold that matters. Jilly doesn't realize that I scribble these present moment thoughts while she is off walking or fixing me coffee or ham sandwiches. She thinks I am organizing my scraps for the next session. She uses a small recorder as I speak of those two days so long ago. And at night, she intends to sit at the kitchen table and transcribe my words with earphones clamped on her head so I won't have to hear my own old voice drifting down the hall to my bedroom.

I see so much, but my eyes grow tired. Soon it will be time. Unci will still be young and still beautiful, and I will be a boy with his pony and his father and grandfathers beside him in a shimmering city.

She comes again, my precious Jilly. I lay aside the cheap green notebook and wait until the hound and the girl come in freshened by light and wind.

Day One

Afternoon Recording Session

"Are you ready then, Jilly."

"Yes, Grandfather."

"Then push your magic buttons there."

I followed Tilde and Grandfather down the blue satin path, shifting in my body from boy to youth to boy again. I was all ages and I was ageless. Once my spine curled like an old oak branch, and I walked as though I were an ancient, bent old man. Above me, the sky was a violet cloudbank like no color I have ever seen in life. It vibrated with light the way clouds grab particles in a sandstorm and hold them, turning the light outward.

Where are we going? Where am I? My silent questions turned and twisted like branches down a flooded river. But I was not anxious or afraid, not until I began to

21

wonder again if I was dead, if I had tumbled off my old horse and died there beneath the cottonwoods.

I thought of my Mamma…

The gray net began to fall around my shoulders, and I flicked my hand like I'd seen my Grandfather do and the grayness flew off again. I was feeling rather proud of this small feat and looked up at Unci and Grandfather to see if they had noticed. They were a ways ahead of me on the path and I blinked twice and looked again. My Unci's hair was now a vivid red. I chuckled. My Unci a redhead? How silly was that. I rushed ahead until I caught up. "Grandfather, why is Unci's hair red now? She's an Indian."

Grandfather snorted, didn't even turn around. "Color is ever-changing here. Haven't you noticed, boy? Tilde has no attachment to being Indian. It's a cap we wear and only for a moment, only for a moment. You'll learn this when we meet with the old ones. *Indian* is the least of who you are."

When he said those words, the air sucked out of my lungs as if I'd been shoved into a vacuum chamber. I was suddenly gasping, terrified, wondering if it was possible for a person to die when they were already in the realm of the dead. Grandfather stopped and clapped me hard on the back between the shoulder blades as if I were choking on a hot dog. "Breathe boy. It's only a spasm. It'll pass. This happens every time we must face our illusions of identity."

I looked at Unci and the red had flown out of her hair like cardinals taking flight. It was a dark braided rope again. "What is he saying, Unci? We *are* Indian."

"Yes, dear, but we are also more—so much more. Never mind now, the Wind will explain. Look, we are here."

My breathing eased and I looked up. The blue satin path we'd been following shifted to silver gray and rose up before me like ground fog and then transformed itself into a stormy looking gray wall. Watching it rise before me made me dizzy, and I lost my balance for a moment. Now a solid-looking gray wall stood before me like the picture of a Norman castle I'd seen once. An arched doorway was cut into the stone, and we entered into the room of the Wind where I was to take my first full lesson. Suddenly, I stood alone in a cavernous hall. Grandfather and Unci had disappeared.

I looked around. The walls rose around me like thunderclouds or smoke yet they appeared solid as well. In front of me was a small, bony, dark-haired man. I couldn't determine his age.

"Greetings," he said, extending his hand.

I took the hand, noticed its cool, leathery feeling. "Who are you?"

He smiled, showing a set of perfectly white teeth, which appeared to glow against the dark lips and face. "I am First Man of the Wind. Come. Rest. We will talk." He squatted to sit, and by the time his bottom met the ground, all around us had shifted again. Now it appeared that we were in a small forest clearing, a friendly fire crackling not twelve inches from First Man's feet. I smelled smoke. This constantly changing landscape was making me sick to my stomach. I squeezed my eyes shut almost fearful of opening them and having the scene shift once again, adding to my vertigo. The man waited to speak until my dizziness had passed, and I could again focus my eyes on him.

"How is it you have come to the realm of the ancestors?" he asked.

"I don't know. I was angry, riding my horse like a maniac one moment and here the next. I don't understand."

First Man nodded. "People travel from your realm usually for one of two reasons. They seek someone—or they have a question."

I smiled. "Can it be for both reasons?"

"Yes, it can. Tell me."

I am not a talker. I especially was not a talker at that age. Normally, I swallowed all my words and pain as if they were small stones until I had a belly full. Booze was all I knew that could make a belly full of stones livable. But there, before the blue flame of First Man's fire, I talked. By my estimation in this strange realm, I talked for twenty hours, one hour for each year of my miserable life. It was like puking, this talk. I told First Man how my people suffer, a river of suffering. I told him the whole story, how the white man came and killed the buffalo and then killed us with disease, with guns, with starvation, with stealing land, with whiskey. He still kills us, I told First Man, now with commodities, with courts, and sometimes, with kindness. Then I told him that he doesn't need to kill us any longer because now we kill each other—or ourselves. I realized as the words spewed forth that my inner volcano had finally erupted. Ash and debris had flowed out all around me and left me empty in the center of a deep cold crater.

I was empty. And it was this emptiness I feared more than anything, even death. I looked at First Man and said, "If you take away my anger, I will have nothing."

He said nothing. I waited in the silence and the emptiness. The fire crackled still. It had not changed in the long day of my talking even though no one added

25

wood or tended it. I looked around actually expecting to see in the landscape around me a land burned and buried in the hot flow of lava. It had not changed either except in the far, far distance I could hear the low thrum of a drum coming from deep in the forest. The sound made me want to weep. I could hear squirrels chattering, birds singing, and all seemed to sing to the drum. "What is that?" I asked First Man.

"It is not our concern. Not yet."

His mysterious answer puzzled me, but I set my curiosity aside and sat up straighter. The emptiness was becoming familiar, not so fearful. "I come for both reasons. I want to ask why all of the killing? And I seek my father."

"Yes, of course," was all he said. He stared into the flame for a long, long time and then he began to talk.

First Man talked for twenty hours. I don't know why I have these specific times in my mind. There was no sun rising and setting, no sense of thirst, hunger, or the need for rest. There were no clocks or watches, no morning birds or late night howl of coyote or wolf. Only the thrumming sound gathering around me and yet I *must* say he spoke for twenty hours.

It was during First Man's twenty hours of talking that the empty crater of my being filled up with his story of

The Wind of a Thousand Years. Since that time, I have spent my life recalling all the details of what he told me. Now I recount it here as best I can. First Man of the Wind is the keeper of that story. He is also a Watcher.

"Ah, Jilly, dear. I am so tired. Can we begin again tomorrow?"

"Of course, Grandpa. We have all the time we need. You rest. I'll go fix us some chicken breasts and broccoli for supper."

Albert's Notes

I sit in my chair, the old favorite recliner, not the new one the grandkids bought me last Christmas. Only Hound Dog and Fat Cat take turns sitting in that brand new chair. Pity. I keep telling them I don't need anything but they continue to bring gifts and try to make me more comfortable. They are dear to me—these grandchildren and great grandchildren.

I can hear Jilly in the kitchen frying the chicken breasts. She is good to come and help me with this. She brings me food but never treats me like a child because I am old. Some people talk to old people as if they were blind, deaf, and stupid. There is not a damn thing wrong with me that death won't take care of. But that has been the true test for me my whole life—when faced with fools, to remember the Wind and what it did, and why. But now, I run ahead of my story. This story, like no other, must be told in order.

Day Two

Morning Recording Session

Albert's Notes

I slept last night without a wiggle. I thought the telling of my vision would bring the dreaming back, but it hasn't, not yet. After my two-day journey, I gave up the booze, but I like my morning coffee to kick a little. Jilly knows that and comes in, hot mugs in hand, looking like the morning star.

"What are you writing, Grandfather," she asked.

"None of your business." I tell her.

She laughs and her laughter clears the morning air of night. She sips her coffee and waits for me to finish writing whatever it is that is none of her business. Jilly knows I bark but I don't bite, like Hound Dog. Before I speak I want to remind my granddaughter and others that these are not my words. I am not wise, despite my great age, and I certainly wasn't wise enough at age twenty to make up First Man's story. I tell it as it was told to me. I have learned that when there is

29

true wisdom in the world, it always comes from the other realms—
and not from the minds of men or women. They have only heard it.

"Are we turned on, Jilly?"

"Yes, Grandfather. We're turned on."

This is First Man's story.

My name is First Man of the Wind of a Thousand
Years. I am from the realm of the ancestors. There are
other worlds, other realms, and I don't speak for them
except to say that the Wind originated there. We, like those
still in the land of the living, are subject to the power of
this great wind.

I was a boy, living in what you know as the southwest
when first I felt the Wind. I lived a simple life with my
parents, my people. We existed much as we had lived from
the first memories that came down to us from our
ancestors in the stories that we kept. It was my favorite
time of day, the time of hearing my parents and
grandparents tell the stories of my people, stories of
spiders weaving, and of my people climbing up through
the realms to emerge on earth as First People. I listened
carefully as I was instructed to do so that one day the
stories could be passed down in a good way to my children
and grandchildren. It was inconceivable that anything

would happen to change that long, slow, unfolding history—until the Wind came.

With the first kiss of this mighty Wind came the drought. In just a few years our lands were sucked dry of all moisture and food was scarce. The people began to break into small groups and travel out from our main village. The hot dry sun baked the earth into crust and the people began to protect food instead of share it. Angers rose and the people built weapons with which to defend themselves, and the peaceful way we had lived for thousands of years was shattered.

One day another tribe came from the south and attacked my family's village. Their storm was violent and quick. When the dust settled, my small body lay on the ground, broken, bloodied, sandwiched between the dead bodies of my parents and surrounded by my dead village. Death was all around. This event so shocked my young spirit that it left my body and fled to the high rock pinnacles surrounding the dead village and perched there, staring down at the horrible sight below. I sat, still and unmoving, watching as the carrion birds and the wild dogs cleaned the bones below.

The sun rose and fell, rose and fell for decades until it had bleached the bones white and still I sat. I didn't know enough to travel alone to the ancestors and none came to

31

claim me. It was not known to me until much later that this long period of stillness, perched and waiting, was my initiation into becoming a Watcher. I also didn't know that in other parts of the world similar terrible events were unfolding and being witnessed by other Watchers across the earth.

The Wind of a Thousand Years had begun.

First Man was a tiny, sinewy little man. It was easy for me to picture the boy's spirit perched on a rock like a bird watching the land below while his spirit aged. Waiting. Watching. The story of his family evoked images of my own family, my own people scattered across the frozen land at Wounded Knee. I did not think I was going to like First Man's story. And I don't, even to this day, although I understand its meaning.

First Man's Story

Eventually, the rock on which I perched began to grow. It rose so high above the earth that soon I could see other nations of people living on other lands. I could see far south into wet jungle lands and torrid areas. I could see north to frozen, icy lands where the bands of people were small clusters moving across snow and ice in their fight to survive the harsh land. I could see east and west, across great bodies of water to other lands. Everywhere I cast my eyes, the people were moving, walking, walking out across the land. As my perch grew higher yet, my eyes could no longer see the bare bones of my parents but only the travelers which I later came to know as The Walkers. I no longer shivered, no longer curled into my spirit body but looked out. And as I looked out, I grew curious at the massive, moving bodies of people.

I wanted to understand what was happening. My questions grew, just as yours have, Albert. Finally, I stood high up on my rocky perch, raised my arms up to the heavens and prayed. It was the first time in all the years of watching I had prayed to the ancestors to show me what was happening.

And then, a miracle. They came for me. The ancestors came and took me home, much the same as they came to get you and for a similar reason—to teach me how to see.

Oh Jilly, the question I asked First Man then still embarrasses me, and I hate to have you record it but don't shut the machine off. Not yet. I must say it. I asked First Man, "Why me? Why have I been chosen to hear your story?"

His answer was simple. "So that you will also become a Watcher. One day, you will translate to the other people what you have seen and heard.

I was sharply aware that I did not want to be a messenger—a Watcher as First Man called it. There was no desire in me to translate unknown things. I was a young man—no, a boy. I wanted no such responsibility. Look at how I had treated my mother, and how I had failed at being the man she needed me to be. Look at how I had failed my sisters, my father, and my people by being drunk and angry. No, I was not a reliable messenger.

First Man seemed to read my mind. "You have chosen it, Albert. It has not chosen you."

When he said those words, I remembered. In quick, flickering scenes I saw that I had crossed many times already between the spirit realms and the earthly realm—in my dreams and thoughts, in my childhood fancies of flying and traveling, in my questioning and in my running away. And certainly, death was not unfamiliar to me. The death of my father, which I had felt so keenly, was just one of many deaths that had pushed my spirit up on to the high peaks to watch and wait, just as First Man had watched and waited. I had, in my spirit, already been a Walker—in training to be a Watcher.

It was my father's death that had finally pushed me into this realm while still holding my broken body in life, at least I hoped that was so—that my body beneath the grove of trees was still waiting for my return. I had chosen it.

To First Man, I said nothing, just nodded to let him know I understood and that he should continue his story. When I gave him that nod, another layer of understanding filled my mind.

I understood that First Man, too, had chosen this. He too had jumped in and out of many lives, many bodies, even while a part of his spirit remained high on a perch above earth. Like him, I knew that my spirit was also perched on a high point and had been watching the progress of my many lives. This, probably, was the first real lesson I got during the twenty hours of speaking, and the next twenty hours of listening.

I must speak this clearly. I had believed, if I thought of it at all as a twenty-year-old, that one body contains only one spirit, rather like a body is given one portion of arms, another portion of eyes and ears. Never had I understood that spirit was a fluid thing, that spirit could be simultaneously in the body and perched high above the earth or perhaps even split and living other lives in other lands.

I am not sure if First Man taught me this or if I just finally understood it. Our way of communicating had gone beyond words, rather like ink in water, one blending into the other. I said to him, "So, you were taken to this realm in a similar way?"

First Man smiled at the way I tried to tie his story down like a pony to a stake. "Yes, I was taken into the council of Elders. They told me of the cycle of learning, that each of us must complete this cycle, but that mankind as a whole must also complete the cycle. And that is why the Winds have come. The Wind of a Thousand Years has come to scatter the many tribes of people into one another so humankind can complete one cycle and begin another. You see, when each cycle ends, a new one begins. Over thousands of years it forms a spiral—not a circle.

First Man was speaking slowly and watching me. He explained that the spiral of life always contains four movements and these four movements coincide with the natural forces of heaven and earth. There are four directions, four seasons, four parts of each day, and that the closing of one cycle opens another. He brushed a place in the dirt and took a stick and drew a circle, but just as he was about to close the circle he skipped past the connecting point and began a spiral.

"You see?" he asked.

I nodded and said, "Yes, I see."

"Good. Each movement has its own energy, a force contained within it that drives the spiraling out. The four energies are gathering, belonging, separating, and aloneness."

Whatever I expected in this great teaching, it was not the four simple words that First Man spoke. I must have looked like the wind blew me over because First Man laughed so hard he rolled onto the ground holding his sides. That was the only time I wondered if a great hoax was being played on a poor drunk kid who couldn't stay atop his horse. I couldn't possibly have gone through all this, yanked into the spirit world to be given such a school boy lesson—gathering, belonging, separating and aloneness?

Finally, First Man quit laughing and came back to our small circle of firelight. "Sorry," he said. "The look on your face, it reminded me of my own reaction when I got the same lesson. These four movements within the spiral contain the natural world—and the wider realms as well. Pick up that stone, Albert."

I looked around and saw no stone. Then I looked again, and we were in a circle of small, smooth stones as white as snow or sugar candy. I was getting used to the fluid ways of this reality. I picked up one of the stones and held it. It felt good, as though it belonged there in my hand.

"Now, let it go again." First Man said.

Oddly, I was reluctant to let it go, but did as I was told. My hand was empty once again.

"You see," said First Man. "You take it up, hold it but a moment, let it go again, and your palm is empty once more." He must have seen my confusion again. "Don't make it a difficult lesson, Albert. It is simple. We gather, hold a moment, let go, and are alone again. You came from the spirit world, you gathered or were bonded into a family, you stayed awhile, then you moved off to find your aloneness once again. The cycle is endless. Everything we take, everything we bind ourselves to we must eventually release and stand alone again."

"I don't understand, First Man. What does this have to do with the Wind—or with life?"

"It has everything to do with the Wind and with life. Do you remember why you came here?"

"To find my father."

"Yes, because you could not separate, could not bear to be alone. This is the breath of life, coming in, staying a moment, releasing, and then going out again to re-gather."

A deep silence settled around us. The thrumming of the drum stopped, the animals ceased their chatter, and the very air around me seemed to stall. I thought hard about First Man's words. In the edge of my vision, a gray pall began to descend. "But to be alone, First Man, it is unbearable."

"Yes, it is. And to be permanently bound, held to one place or person, it too is unbearable."

I was silent, staring into the flames. In the moving light of the flame I saw scenes unfold, of an infant letting go of the womb in his slide into life, the child letting go of its mothers hand, a boy letting go of his father's bleeding body—gathering, belonging, separating, and aloneness.

First Man nodded. "You see, all are necessary in the wider movement of life. All are equally powerful forces. And what is true for the single soul is true for the greater soul. A cycle is closing on earth now, Albert, and it is necessary that the human race see this cycle and accept it now if they are to survive as a species."

"Jilly?"

"Yes, Grandfather?"

"Are you okay?"

"What did he mean, Grandfather? If we are to survive as a species?"

"It will become clear, my dear girl. But first, a break now."

Albert's Notes

I had seen the shiver enter Jilly's body from First Man's words. When I looked up from my many scraps of paper, her eyes had become wide, dark disks in her face. Oh, how I longed to wrap these old arms around her young self, but knew that is not what I had been instructed to do. These intense moments, of awakening from dream, from sleep, from illusion were exactly what we need now, in this moment. We need to feel the truth of First Man's words. We cannot freeze the cycle without freezing life itself. There is no need to fear your aloneness, Jilly, I told her. It contains the greatest of all gifts. It is in alone that we enter the next cycle, the gathering. I think you sociology students call it 'bonding'. I rather like the word gathering, myself."

She was not listening to me. Her soul had retreated to its own tall peak to scan the landscape below. Jilly knew about alone. Both of her parents had died of alcoholism before she was ten. She had lived with me for a decade, and with an auntie since. When she was first born I had had a vision of Jilly, and so I knew her soul. I knew her aloneness would make her a Watcher, that one day she would lead others to the high places of earth where they could see clearly. I trusted that vision. Go. Take a break, Jilly. I need to gather my thoughts, I told her. I must have sounded a bit abrupt. Her feelings played across her face like winter skies. How difficult it is not to sooth, not to say more to ease her pain. She went quietly off and wandered out the front door into the sunshine. I smiled again to myself. She knows from which direction her strength came.

For years after my journey into the spirit realm, I had forgotten this part of First Man's story. Then one day I witnessed a tornado off in the distance traveling over the earth, hovering a moment, placing its pointed toe on the earth, and flying off again to the north. It had looked like a great being, and then I remembered. The spiral. It has a tiny point of gathering at the base and then moves out in a whirling twist to the top. It catches it all and moves it up and out. I think First Man must have sent that tornado to remind me.

Day Two

Afternoon Recording Session

"Another day, Jilly. Are we ready?"

"Yes, Grandfather. I'm ready."

"So I continue with First Man's story."

First Man spent many hours recounting the ways in which the cycle of gathering, belonging, separating, and aloneness play out in the world. Think of the seasons—the way warmth and earth gather around seeds in spring, carry them in the cradle of belonging through summer to full bloom, and then the slow separating movement of fall followed by a withdrawal into winter—alone.

Winter is the longest season, he said, a time of the dimmest sunlight, the hibernation prior to the beginning of a new cycle. It is longest, perhaps, because it is the most important. It is the deep rest and preparation needed for the next great gathering of energy, the energy that brings life and heat.

First Man walked me through many such cycles beginning with conception of the human child, when the seed of mother and father gather and bond, linger in the womb for many months, and then end with the shocking separation of mother and child at birth when the next cycle/spiral begins. In this cycle we are child, adult and then elder until we descend into death—and aloneness—once again. The cycles, both large and small, are continuous.

He spoke of the rain, the gathering of moisture, one particle bonding with another, the holding of clouds and sky, the letting go of a rainstorm, and the still, quiet of aloneness when the cycle prepares to begin again. In all the living kingdoms, the cycles play out in the four movements. He said we act as if there were only birth and death without the balance of all four forces working together to bring about each birth, each death.

First Man showed me the presence of the four powerful forces of the universe in a dozen different ways. Finally, when he was sure I understood, he rose. As he stood, the friendly fire was instantly gone, and we stood now in an emerald green valley. He smiled at me. "Creation is fun, isn't it?"

This was an understatement. It was magnificent in this realm of light and shadow and shifting forms.

"Let's walk." First Man said. "I will show you what the wind has done, and then I will tell you why."

It is difficult to recount that walk. In terms of physical distance, it was no more than a single mile, and yet we traveled through centuries of time across all the continents of earth. He showed me first the tribes of Africa and those he called *The Walkers*. It was here, he told me, that man first left what he called *First Family*.

"You see, Albert. Your people have one small memory from that time. People forget to remember and when something drifts into memory, they remember to forget."

First Man seemed to be enjoying his word play. My mind was repeating, "forget to remember—remember to forget" in a confusing swirl, and yet it made sense.

We reached a high hillside and First Man stopped. He waved a hand out across the open space and the scene shifted. Suddenly, I saw all the lands and all the tribes in a single instant. A great wind came from all four directions simultaneously like a giant dust devil. In what seemed a mere blink of time, the wind scattered all the tribes of earth into one another. It was an astounding sight. These were not the Walkers of First Family we had seen, but all the families, and clans, and tribes that came after.

I stood on that hillside and witnessed a windstorm of people blowing across the land like dry leaves. Some of the movements I remembered from childhood history classes. The Romans blew into Britain, the British blew into Africa and India, and the Indians, Chinese, and Asians blew across the planet. The pale leaves of Europe blew in great gusts across the ocean and out across the vast lands of North America, and then the Africans blew out of Africa and landed in their midst. There were other nations blowing in from other corners of earth that I couldn't recognize. Small groups and large all tumbling together across earth. No nation was untouched from what I could see, and no century free of the blast of this mighty Wind.

From our high perch, it appeared to be a colorful and lively chaos. But in my soul, I knew it was a bloody chaos, a chaos that soaked the earth with the lifeblood of millions upon millions of lives, including my Grandma Tilde, including my father. I saw no such small detail, but I knew.

First Man stood beside me and said nothing. He just let me watch the Wind blow across the earth until it felt as though it surrounded me, sucking the very breath out of my lungs once again.

I gasped, grew short of breath, and finally fell to my knees watching that Wind do its terrible job. I wanted to cry out to First Man, "Why? Why this terrible destruction? Why is it necessary?" But there was no breath in my lungs with which to form the words. I thought of the cruel god of my youth, the god that would allow such devastation to visit his children. My bones ached, and my skin felt pricked by needles—or by the wind.

The gray net fell around my shoulders and thickened into a heavy blanket that threatened to suffocate me. I groped in the darkness of this despair, a despair like none other I had known. I could no longer see or hear First Man or see the points of light flashing across a beautiful land. Never, ever, have I felt so alone. I was under the blanket for hours, a hundred years, a lifetime or more. It knitted its edges around me like a thick cocoon. It became a sack in which nothing could enter and nothing could escape.

To keep from going insane in such a dark womb, I curled more deeply into myself and listened to the nearly inaudible thump, thumping of my own heart. It grew louder in my ears, reminding me of the slow thrum of a large ceremonial drum. The sound comforted me, and I let it surround me. The thump, thump became the center of my universe, the center of my being. It grew stronger,

47

steadier and then the sound itself became like a presence, something outside of my body, something with substance and weight. There is no explanation for what I experienced, but the presence gently, slowly, absorbed my fear, taking it from me in small bites, swallowing it into the thump, thump. My body began to feel light and then lighter still. In some mysterious way it became light. Each cell of my body became a glowing orb until I exploded with light and the cocoon of gray flew off.

Rubbing my arms and legs, I sat up and looked out at the world that lay before me. First Man was nowhere to be seen. I was alone. I crossed my legs Indian style. I was very calm. Perhaps for the first time in my short twenty years I felt as smooth as a lake on a windless July day. I took a deep breath. The air was sugar-scented, like walking by the cotton candy booth at the county fair. The forming and reforming points of energy seemed made of light—and sugar.

I looked down into the valley where the ferocious Winds had blown the human leaves of the world into one another, and now instead of death, blood, and destruction, the entire valley was filled with a standing grove of sturdy, tall trees of all varieties. It was magnificent. For some reason, the sight of those pine, birch, poplar, elm, and oak standing together cracked my frozen heart, and I dropped my face into palms and wept. I wept and wept until my tears formed streams, and then rivers of water flowing out from where I sat. My tears flowed across the land and watered the trees. A slight breeze blew in from the south and stirred the many living leaves and needles and seedlings, and I felt the *wopila*, the thanksgiving, of the trees for my generous tears.

Albert's Notes

I had to smile when I looked up from telling this part of my story. Jilly's cheeks were raining tears. So were mine. I smiled when my tears dropped from my face and landed on the pages resting in my lap.

"We are a pair, aren't we Jilly, my girl?" I said to her.

"Oh, Grandfather..."

"Love." I told Jilly. "It was love that allowed me to see the grove of trees, so strong and resilient, and not the leaves and the blowing Winds. First Man didn't' need to be there to explain what I had experienced. I went deeply into my despair, into my aloneness, into my darkness, and emerged only with love. Reborn in love. I need to rest now Jilly. Soon, tomorrow, we will return to the grove and what I learned there."

"Yes Grandpa."

When Jilly left, I leaned my head back and thought again of the message of that standing grove with its roots so firmly dug into the earth. That image, amid all the other images from my visit to the other realm, has remained the most visible, the most beautiful, the most meaningful. I have spent fifty years understanding this meaning, and in the hundreds of books, lectures, and classes that I took following that fateful fall from my horse, none gave more than that image. I learned to spot the other Watchers instantly. I knew how to recognize others who had seen the standing grove and who knew it was the only possible future for our human race.

Day Three

Morning Recording Session

"Are you ready then?"

"Yes, Grandpa, but can I tell you something first?"

"Of course, as long as it doesn't lead me too far ahead in my story."

"No, it won't. It is, well, I keep thinking about what you said about remembering to forget and all that. It is the weirdest thing. I've been transcribing your tapes at night, but when I listen to the tape, I find I have forgotten all you said. Isn't that strange? Why can't I remember? I heard it only a couple of hours before."

"You must think you are getting as old as your grandfather. No, Jilly. It isn't so strange. This story, as I have told you, is not mine but comes from the other realm. Because we are here, in these so human bodies, the material from the other realms is a shifting, changing thing easily caught in the web of forgetting. Not to worry, pretty girl. Not to worry. The right parts of the story will come to you at the right time. You will see."

"All right, Grandfather. I trust you're right.

"It is what I hope for, Jilly, that in telling this story the words will be like rain and tears and pure enough to wash the thin veil of gray from our eyes so we can see— and remember. Now, to the task at hand, is your little machine ready to remember?"

"Yes, it is more reliable than I am. Go."

I was still staring into the valley of trees when First Man walked up behind me. He put a hand on my shoulder and asked, "Do you see the power of alone?"

"Yes. It is not a lonely thing, not if we release the fear." I was strangely comforted by his hand at my shoulder, his presence behind me. I recognized that the new cycle begins with the gathering of strength and energy.

"Yes, if we release the fear and listen for the deeper rhythm of things. Come with me now. You are ready for the next lesson."

I followed First Man as he walked a path down the mountain and into the valley that held the standing grove of trees. My ears still heard the deep thump, thump that had restored my sanity. Beneath my feet the soil was damp and I smiled. My tears. First Man was silent as we walked.

My sense of seeing, hearing, tasting, smelling were vibrating in this vivid world. I didn't want words, only this wide-awake thing flashing around me. When we had walked for perhaps an hour, we came to a grove of aspen trees lacing their thin stumps and branches through the other, sturdier pine and oak. We came to a small clearing and First Man stopped. "You're classroom."

I laughed, for sitting in the center of the clearing was a small, wooden desk very much like the kind we had in the mission school. It sat ridiculously alone and out of place in the peaceful, leafy grove. I fully expected a black-garbed nun or priest to step out from behind a tree.

"You like it?" First Man grinned at me.

"Funny, First Man. I think I will call you Funny Man."

"I like it, too." First Man waved a hand and the hard, wooden desk disappeared in a flash of dissolving points of light. "Do you know, Albert, that an aspen grove is one of the largest and oldest living organisms on earth?"

"No, I didn't."

"Yes, beneath the earth their roots are common roots. This whole grove of aspen trees is one family. It can travel when it runs low of food and water. Do you know why it is so long-lived?"

"No." I felt as though I should take a seat in the little wooden desk.

First Man walked over to one of the trees and spanned its trunk with his ten fingers as if it were the waist of a pretty girl. "This tree knows to whom it belongs. It never forgets. All the trees, they stand alone, are separate, and yet they hold their belonging deep within their roots. This pretty aspen will never wonder if it should be a pine or a maple. It is an aspen."

"What are you saying, First Man?" It seemed obvious to me, but I knew he wanted me to see a deeper meaning in his words.

"Let's sit. I want to tell you about the four ages of humankind."

I sat, as instructed, and First Man talked and talked for many hours again. I cannot recount all his words but will retell the lesson as I understand it. He said again that the cycle of gathering, belonging, separating, and aloneness is both a very small cycle and part of a larger spiral. Just as day passes into night, and summer passes into winter, and life passes into death, each cycle is both separate and part of the larger spiral of life. We are all subject to the same natural law. The human race, First Man explained, has been in one singular sweep of this spiral for thousands of years, since the first Walkers walked out across the earth and left the First Family. While continuing in their small ways to form tribes and clans, and dissolve tribes and clans in order to form other camps of belonging, they have also been engaged in the first single spiraling loop of consciousness.

First Man said a thousand years ago the gathering, or bond and belong parts of the first large loop was completed and that's when The Wind of a Thousand Years began to blow the people of earth into one another. It is the time of separating, First Man told me, a painful but necessary time, a time of letting go of old identification and attachment, a rite of passage for the species as a whole. A necessary madness, he said. And now, in our time, in my time, we are entering the time of aloneness.

Remember the gray cocoon? First Man told me that most of the human race is now blanketed in this gray. In this time, and probably for another hundred years, the sense of despair, grief, isolation and loneliness will reach its zenith. During that time there will continue to be great suffering and bloodshed. As I listened to his voice, I thought of the many wars even now burning across the earth.

This making of war, he said, is a desperate attempt to find our footing by creating a mythical belonging, a false belonging. It is the noisy claim of one group over another, but is a belonging no longer based in root and seed but in ideology, theology, a belonging of the mind only and not the body. It is the belonging that comes with forgetting.

I didn't like his words. I didn't like the truth of his words. They left me dead and cold in the center of my belly. I felt my old anger rising like a serpent inside, of Indian and white, of rich and poor, the unfairness of it all. I wanted there to be no truth in what he said. First Man saw my anger and waited.

"You see," he said, "How quickly we jump to take back our smallest identity."

"But you said it yourself. This aspen is an aspen—not a pine or maple or elm."

"Stop, Albert. Remember the standing grove. And remember the aspen is the oldest living organism, and the wisest. It never cuts its own roots."

I did remember, but struggled to understand as if it were a difficult math problem.

First Man smiled. "You are young, Albert. You will not get this all in grade school. There is time." With that he turned and began following the path down which we had entered the grove. When he began the upward climb, however, he took a path toward the east as best as I could tell. The land was still beautiful but I noticed it had lost its sweet sugar smell.

"My energy leaves me again, Jilly, and I need a break."

"Yes, Grandfather. I'll make us some lunch."

"Thank you, dear. And don't despair—the best is yet to come."

Albert's Notes

I smiled a bit at myself. Don't despair? We are in the era of despair. I may as well tell the sun not to shine or the moon not to bother rising.

While Jilly makes us a nice lunch of tuna fish, I wander back to my room and sit on the edge of my bed. I stare out across this sun-drenched land. It is a relief to finally be finishing what was begun so long ago. I no longer fear death. It holds little interest except as it opens that next spiral of gathering, belonging, separating, and aloneness. Jilly calls me to lunch.

I take a long sip of the coffee she brings me. It is warm and creamy, a little sweetened. I like to crush a cardamom seed in it with a sprinkle of cinnamon, an old recipe I learned from a man from India. He came all across the world to see what we Lakota mean by We are all related. We became friends and spent many pleasant hours comparing and contrasting our two separate traditions, our spiritual beliefs, and concluded they were more similar than separate.

Jilly leaves me to enjoy my coffee and review my notes for this afternoon's session and here my mind has drifted off to India, and to a grove of aspen trees. I thought a long time about what First Man said about the aspen and how they never cut their roots; that is why they are so long lived.

I understood the need for common roots, or at least I thought I did. But I was unable to reconcile the earlier images of many leaves blowing around the world, all different colors, and all different races.

At first I thought the white-barked aspen must mean First Man was talking about white people, and that we must all maintain our racial identity if we were to survive as a race. The pine must be a pine, the aspen an aspen. Finally, many decades later what First Man said began to make sense. The whole human race is one family, like the aspen, linked at the root, traveling over the world, always related, always connected. The other trees—the pine, the elm, the oak—those are other families.

Day Three

Afternoon Recording Session

"The coffee is good this afternoon, Jilly."

"Thanks, Grandpa. Are you ready?"

"Yes. Stop me, *takoja*, if what I say is not clear. I want to get this next part down in a good way. Are we on?"

"Yes."

"Good."

The era of despair. First Man said the end of each major cycle commingles with the opening of the next. One is closing, another opening but not like doors, not so clearly defined. He explained that during this long transition, there will appear to be very different types of humans on earth. The time of transition will be blurred, and there will be difficult struggles as the long dark winter is ending and a new spring beginning.

First Man said several things would influence whether we survive as a race or simply blink out of all time. Most importantly, he said, we must take our gathering and belonging only from our ancestral line and from the parents. The parents are like the spillway of a great reservoir high in the mountains. Like water spilling over a damn, the flow of life must enter us through the gateways of our parents and from there, we take our truest belonging. We may choose to gather with others and belong, but it is only fleeting and temporary except for the ancestral line. We must strengthen our clans and follow the line of memory and learning through these pathways.

If we do this, if we create strong families, from these sturdy cradles will spring the new child. First Man was very particular about this. This child, rooted firmly in the family, will remember to remember. This child will see both forward and backward. He called these children *The Weavers*. This child, he said, would be able to see back before the time of the Wind and remember to whom he or she truly belongs. Because they are firmly rooted in the family, like the aspen, they will be strong and have long lives and recognize that there is only one human family.

I asked First Man why he named them so. He said they would be born with the potential to weave one realm with another. With proper care, they will remember the spirit realm from which they came. The Weavers will have access to the higher realms and will therefore have special abilities to hear, to feel, to see beyond the physical body and into the spirit body, wherever it roams. First Man told me we must take great care in the raising of the weaving child, and that I would receive further instructions on that later. It is enough to know that in this new opening of the spiral of gathering, belonging, separating, and alone, the gathering or bonding will be with the higher realms. The Weavers toss the net that makes this possible, the weaving of heaven and earth together into one continuous fabric.

I was entranced with that image of small children weaving threads that tie this earthly life to the higher realms. From my understanding, the Watchers of my age become the Weavers in this new age.

When he had finished his long talk about the Weavers, I asked First Man the question that had been sitting on my breast ever since I came here to this place, perhaps even longer, since I came from the spirit realm as a newborn into my troubled family. He'd told me earlier that I chose it, it did not choose me, but I needed to ask, "Why me, First Man?"

He looked at me for a long moment and then smiled. "Ah, that ancient question. Where would humankind be without that question?"

First Man began to turn away but I was not to be put off. "I need to know. Why have you brought me here? Why have you told me of the spiral of life?"

"You forget so quickly, Albert. We did not bring you here. You came because of your question—and to find your father."

"But I haven't found my father."

Then, in the odd manner of this realm, the moving points of light and energy rearranged themselves within the bird-like body of First Man. His flesh filled, his skeletal frame shifted before my eyes and, in a moment, First Man was my father. He said nothing, just stood before me with the steely strength I remembered so well.

"Father."

"My son."

I was stunned to be looking into the eyes of my father. Around me points of light flickered with remembered images. They came very fast—Father putting me on a pony, Father teaching me to hunt, Father cornering Mother to steal a kiss, Father wiping morning milk from my sister's mouth. The poisonous pain and grief that had so filled me to the brim two years ago when he died rushed to my head. I nearly passed out, and deep within my belly grief rolled up my body like thunder. Suddenly an astounding sound issued from my mouth that

64

was both human and animal, both call and cry. I couldn't stop it. It was as if the wailing became like great birds that clutched my pain and hurt in their sharp talons, and then flew out of my body.

Father took me in his arms and held me. I couldn't speak. There was nothing to say. He cradled my speechless body until the wailing ceased and only a breathless gasping issued from my mouth. I grew calm again, resting deeply in his care. A bright, new sun rose in my body as I realized first, that he had not ever been gone from me, not where it counts, and second, that my strength was in my roots. Just as First Man had said, my true belonging was to him and to my mother's line and then to the line of my human family. In order to be strong in the world I needed to know that.

Finally, my grief—and my great relief—was exhausted. I pulled away from him and smiled at this man who had given me life from the seed of his body. "I found you."

Father shook his head. "I was not lost. You were. What you found was yourself, Albert. Come. Let's sit."

We chose a large boulder and sat in the sun. I wanted to know the connection between the man I knew as my father and First Man, who had showed me the story of The Wind of a Thousand Years.

"There is no need to tell you all of my stories, son. The many times my spirit has traveled from this realm to the others is like a man crossing a streambed. First on one bank, then into the water, then up onto the far bank. You also have been in and out like a frog in a pond." He chuckled and the sound warmed my soul. "We all have. Most of us are blessed with not having to remember. We are all traveling the same spiral." He stopped a moment and cocked his head as if listening or testing the wind. "We must finish this talk soon. You cannot leave your physical body for so long that it is damaged or dies."

At first I laughed. I'd grown so accustomed to this place I'd nearly forgotten the young, drunk Albert beneath another standing grove. But then the laughter died and a flood of shame brought the gray net hovering over my head. "I haven't been a very good son, father."

"I know, son."

"I am ashamed."

"It will be better now. Not easy, but better. There is much that needs to be done. You mustn't replace pain and anger with guilt. Guilt is a useless thing unless we learn."

"But what am I to do? What is the meaning of all of this?"

"The lessons have been clear. They will become even clearer as you age. One day, when the time is right, you are to give these lessons away. You are in your own small cycle, son. You are gathering. You will go home and carry these things for many, many years, and then you will set them apart, give them away to others, and you will be alone once again and ready for the next spiral."

"How will I know when the time is right?"

"I can't tell you that. You will know. All I can say is that one day when you are old and nearly ready to come back to this realm, a young woman will come to you. You will give her this story. Write down all you remember from your time here, and all you learn from it as you move through life. Keep it for her."

"Who is she?"

"She is First Man's wife. I call her First Woman. She is part of my story. You see son, we are all part of long story lines. Occasionally, we remember them. Most of the time, we don't. First Woman's story also begins with the coming of the Wind. It is nearly time for you to meet her."

Above my head the sky grew dense and gray. This clouded world was becoming familiar to me, caught by the net of my own fear and doubt. "Father, what if I fail? What if I don't do this in a good way? How will I know?"

"You will know, son. We always know when the path is right. But then we must choose that path. There are other Watchers, many of them now around the world who have been given a similar task. Your part is not so great."

Father must have seen the balloon of my pride deflate a little and he chuckled. "A prophet you're not. Never take this gift in a prideful way. It is the only sure way to fail. Do you understand? You will be silent except with a few guides you will meet along the way, until it is time to complete this moment."

"Yes Father, I understand."

"Also understand that I will not be so far away."

"Thank you, Father." And then I thought of the little desk in the grove and laughed. "Why the school desk?"

Father slapped my shoulder and smiled. "If you would have gone and looked, you would have seen your initials carved into the corner. Come, now you will go to First Woman and get her teachings and then it will be time to return."

There was so much I wanted to ask him, especially about the gunshot, the blood, the death, my mother and sisters, how I would explain to them ... but all the questions fled my mind like nervous sparrows as soon as they landed. It was clearly not the time to ask these questions, and I thought what he said about always knowing the right path. I did, however, keep my eye on my father's back as we walked, fearful that he would vanish in a swirl of moving points of energy. Grief began to rest on my shoulders like a shawl cut from the blanket of gray. Must I lose him a second time, I wondered. Why?

Before we'd walked a quarter mile, father stopped walking and turned back to me, as if he'd sensed the direction of my thoughts. He put his hand on my shoulder and turned my body away from his. "Look again, Albert, out into the great valley to the grove of trees."

I raised my eyes and stared out across the vast lands, my father at my back, his hand resting on my shoulder. He said, "This is my place always. You cannot lose me, just as my father holds his place forever at my back, and his behind him. You must plant this feeling, this energy, deeply into your body and then fear will no longer rule your life."

I stood a long time and did as he told me. I took the radiant heat of his presence behind me and sunk it deep into my belly. As I did this, the fear, the grief, the grayness left once again.

"Good." He said.

I turned, knowing this would be my final full look at the form of my father. "I love you, Father. I hadn't told you that, not for a long time. That was the hardest thing. I never told you."

Father smiled. "You didn't have to."

Albert's Notes

Poor Jilly. This was proving to be an emotional task for her, acting as my secretary. Her cheeks were wet with tears yet again. She, too, had lost her father at a young age. "Come, let me show you."

I took her hand and pulled her to her feet. She had done all of the recording sessions sitting on my floor at my feet. Jilly swiped at her tears with the back of her hand. It made her look six and not twenty-three. We are always a child to our parent or grandparent. I turned her body so she could look out across my golden prairie. and then I stood behind her just as my father had done, my hands resting very lightly on her shoulder, to add presence and not burden. "Close your eyes." I told her. "Now, let your body feel your father behind you, and his father behind him here." I pressed my fingertips against her shoulder. "And on the other side is the line of your mother stretching so far back you see only the haze of time." I pressed my fingertips into her other shoulder. "Your strength comes in here, from behind you, from the strong men and women of your line. It comes to give you courage."

Jilly nodded.

"You feel it?" I asked her.

She nodded again. I felt the subtle shifting of energy, the realignment of her body beneath my palms. I smiled and whispered in her ear. "Now sink it deep." I waited a moment. "Good. Now open your eyes and look out there at our beautiful world. If you look very

71

carefully, you will see the play, the points of light moving, always moving."

When Jilly turned around to face me, she wrapped her arms around my waist and hugged me. "Thank you, Grandpa. I got it. I sunk it deep."

"Wonderful. Maybe we need a short walk. Let's go see if the air out there is made of sugar this morning."

We had a lovely walk and returned to my humble dwelling much refreshed. Jilly cut up some more chicken breasts and we ate one of those dull salads people are so wild about these days. Then I retired to my room to watch the darkness come and the pale light of the moon rise over the earth.

Day Four
Morning Recording Session

"Already this becomes a pattern, Jilly, with you sitting there, and me sipping coffee. Is your machine on?"

"On and recording, Grandfather.

"Good, this is good. We are almost there. Let me see, where did I leave off yesterday?"

In all the time I had spent with First Man, my father, we had been in the beautiful emerald valley, the sun bright and yellow above us. Now, as my father finished his instructions to me, his form again shifted to the smaller, sinewy form of First Man as we neared the top of the hill. The gray walls I'd first encountered with my Grandfather rose suddenly around us once again. They were the color of slate that threw light back at me. I put my hand flat on its surface and it felt as solid as any stonewall I'd felt.

First Man smiled. "Don't worry. It is solid, just not as solid as we once believed."

I entered through the same arched doorway into the wide hall but when I turned to speak to First Man, he was gone. He had not followed me in. Fear clutched my middle for an instant, but the feeling was quickly replaced or removed by that warm presence behind me that my father had told me to sink into my belly. Evidently, I had done it right.

I wandered an open, empty space that looked like a large, enclosed courtyard. Uncertain about what to do next, I waited, but not for long. I felt her presence before she entered. There was a change in the air, a softening of the energy—it's hard to describe, but when I turned to see where the change was coming from, I saw First Woman enter from an opening to my right. I think I had expected a female twin to the sinewy First Man, but instead before me was the most beautiful young women I have ever seen. She was so beautiful, I felt oafish, lumpy, and adolescent in her presence.

Her features were fine and smooth. Long hair flowed to her waist and seemed to take the qualities of this place into itself because the color shifted with each step she took. It was dark as the night sky one moment, a pale red sunrise the next, and then yellow as sunlight a second later.

Finally, all color left until her hair looked like a moon-beam. I must have looked ridiculous, like a boy meeting a movie star. She laughed and I heard bells, crystal bells, tinkling in her laughter.

"Oh Albert." She laughed again. "You look dumbstruck." She ran a hand over her hair as if telling it to settle down, and it muted all color back to deep night.

You would think such a woman would wear flowing white robes but she wore only an ordinary tan cotton shift. No adornment, no rings, no beads, no strands of shell or headgear of feathers. In truth, she needed nothing added. I think I was just a little in love, maybe a lot. Forever after I would seek her in all the women I saw, and would eventually marry the one that had her qualities. I shook myself and blushed. "Sorry. You are First Woman and I am rude. I expected you to be old."

"I am. I am very, very old." She grinned. "Come, we have much to talk about and very little time." First Woman turned and quickly walked out the way she had entered. I followed. We passed the gray walls and were suddenly standing on the shore of a beautiful turquoise lake surrounded by red canyon walls. Across the lake, twin waterfalls flowed over high ledges and landed in limestone-crusted plates of stone that looked placed by the hand of god. A fine misty spray reached my face from where we stood.

First Woman said, "Pretty, isn't it? It is my favorite place in all of the realms. Water helps me think." She walked down the path a hundred yards and sat down on a wide slab of polished wood cut from a giant cottonwood tree. I took a place beside her.

"You are having quite the adventure, Albert."

"Yes."

"I am to instruct you about the Weavers, the children who are arriving. Many are already here, actually."

I had nearly forgotten the words First Man had said, so filled with my father was I still. "Yes, First Man told me."

The bright look on her face faded as though a cloud had passed overhead. I glanced upward but the sky was a sheet of blue.

"You must listen carefully, Albert. Much depends upon these children finding their place in this time. For a thousand years the wind has tumbled the people of earth into one another until they no longer remember where they belong, who they are, or what they have come to do. The longing, the seeking, the deep sense of aloneness and isolation will, for a time yet, cloud all connection with the higher realms, even with the earthly realm. It is a blindness of the soul—you know of what I speak."

"Yes, I think I do." I thought again of blind Albert unconscious beneath a grove of cottonwoods.

"It comes rapidly now, this time of change. Soon you must go back, but my instructions are very specific and won't take long, so I want to tell you one small story from my own storyline." First Woman smiled and the shadow lifted. Her smile warmed me to the core of my being. I really was in love. She could have talked for one hundred years and I would not have wiggled, so enamored of her was I.

"Before the Wind began, actually it was already blowing, we just didn't know it, but all the people had a deep belonging with the natural world. We spoke the language and heard the language of earth, stone, animals, dreams, and the soft whispers from the spirit realm. We spoke the language and we listened. It was a natural, graceful way of being. In truth, we couldn't have survived this cycle without the help of the plants and animals. When the Wind began, it stirred the natural rhythms and disturbed them. It brought with it the beginning energy of separating and, with that, an awareness of what is mine— and what is yours." First Woman stopped and gazed into my face. "Do you understand?"

I wasn't sure.

"The deep harmonies were disturbed, Albert. Now, instead of living in belonging with all things, we drifted from true belonging into ownership. This belongs to me. That belongs to you. That doesn't belong. You see—the energy of belonging shifted."

I nodded, now understanding her meaning.

"It is impossible to describe how this shift interrupted the natural rhythms, but you can see the result in your world. Now, the people of earth fight to have—and not to be. From this place I am now, this high vista, I see the many cycles which form the spiral First Man spoke to you of, the energies of gathering, belonging, separating, and aloneness. Now a new twist of the spiral opens. It will carry humankind into the next and even deeper communication between the realms. But it has been very painful, this ending of one cycle and the opening of the new."

As First Woman spoke, I felt the pain of which she spoke like a knife-point at my throat. I said nothing, just nodded again like a puppet.

"When I was a young girl I, like you, was taken to the other realm, this realm, and made a Watcher. It is difficult to be a Watcher, Albert. You live in one world while simultaneously seeing another. It is confusing, and sometimes very painful. Always you ask why others cannot see what you see. You feel very alone. You see—but are seldom seen by others. Being instructed, as you have been during your time here, helped me but I still had to live in a world that was rapidly changing."

First Woman took my hand in hers and continued. "In my village, a neighbor to the village First Man came from, I was a maiden of the Sun. I took the Sun as my master. Another man, a priest in my village, fell into the Wind and took darkness into his soul. I tell you this not as an indulgence but to let you know that in that time, the seed of this time was also planted. I fled my village with another Watcher from the south. I had twin babies in my womb. The evil priest believed himself to be the father of those babes, a boy and a girl, but in truth, they were special children formed from the mating of the Sun and the Moon."

First Woman gave another tinkling laugh. "Never mind about the logistics of that mating—it simply was. There were others born to the Watchers at that same time around the world. It is these special children who have seeded the human race with what is needed as the new spiral begins. The descendants of all of those children are like a silver net holding the potential for this new time, when the Wind is ending. I'll try to explain in more modern terms. The energy of sun and moon combined in these children created a new chamber in the brain." First Woman tapped her forehead between her brows. "Here. This chamber is not unlike its predecessor, it is the place of connection, of gathering, but in these descendants of sun and moon, it carries an even greater potential, a preparation for the new spiral of gathering and belonging. A wider reach, so to speak."

First Woman was excited about this mysterious chamber of which she spoke. Her eyes were wide and shining. I could not take the time to think through all she said because I simply needed to record her words in my mind so I wouldn't forget.

"Oh, Albert. The potential is so great, so far reaching and full of promise, and yet so fragile at the same time. It is container only. It is like having a miraculous machine but it must first be turned on. It if is properly filled or turned on the human race will flourish once again and surpass its former state of being. The sense of belonging will reach far, far beyond the skin of a single person. Do you understand?"

"I think so." In truth, I didn't understand yet, but her excitement was so contagious that I was caught it its glow.

"The Wind of a Thousand Years will not have been in vain for it will herald in such a time of peace, of connection, of light. I want that for the next generation and all the generations to follow."

Her eyes misted over and pale particles of light and energy rose up from her shining hair again and formed a halo around her head. Such a vision she held for our poor beleaguered race, this human race, and with her help, I saw the promise of it too. Her vision of humanity bloomed in my own mind although it was not the world I currently knew.

She watched my face, her gaze tender and sweet. "You see it?"

"I do."

"Good. Then my story has carried what it needed to carry to you." She leaned over and kissed my brow in the same place she had tapped her own brow. "Now sink it, Albert. Sink that vision into your spirit."

She sounded like my father and I laughed. With that most tender of kisses, First Woman became all business again. She ran quickly through my instructions on what she called 'Care of the container for Weavers.' She began by reminding me that we cannot know which children are descendants of the sun and moon energies and so therefore, the instructions apply to all children. As it should be, she said. She did say that we will in some ways be able to recognize the Weavers because they will enter the world greedy, restless for knowledge, impatient to learn, and intolerant when that learning is denied or constrained.

First Woman then spent a long time talking to me about how in this new time we must be mindful of the larger container of earth. That the Weavers must have pure water, pure air, the food supply restored and cared for, that the ability of these children to weave will depend upon their own brain's ability to weave its fine connections. "Caring for the weaving child requires a larger spiral of care," she said, "That includes care of the mother, care for the family, and care of the earth."

Remember that the man receiving these rapid instructions was a crazy, twenty-year-old youth who had not even considered fatherhood as an option yet. I think that First Woman must have poured the information like liquid into my own container. I took it in whole, in one long, thirsty drink and have never forgotten the simple instructions she gave. Placing these instructions into the world that unfolded as I grew and aged was another matter entirely. From what I could see, in the final decades of apathy and despair, our institutions and culture did exactly the opposite of what she instructed. It was remarkable.

But I also saw that these children with the golden chambers, the special containers, would not be denied the learning or the care required.

"A break, Jilly? I begin to stray from my story."

"Yes, Grandpa."

Albert's Notes

Jilly looked reluctant to push the stop button on her recorder but smiled. Oh, I knew she was one of them, one of the Weavers. I haven't yet said a word about the others, the ones not descended from this ancient line, born of sun and moon, the ones whose containers, for whatever reason, were not filled with this potential.

First Woman called them The Weepers. Sadly, those who could not pass through the final days of the Wind, she said, would cry all their lives for what they could not have, be, or do. They would die having never thrown off the gray net of despair. I will make no further mention of this hereafter. You will know them when you meet them, the Weepers. They cry and they cry. First Woman also told me to remember that eventually all will cross the stream again and be descendants of sun and moon.

For many years I wondered about this use of words beginning with a 'W' in this language of the other realms, and the new spiral. The only thing I saw is that it is the only letter in the English alphabet whose two thin arms reach for heaven, for the higher realms, while its two feet are firmly planted on the earth. 'W'. Firmly seated—but reaching.

The telling of this story, so long held, is both energizing and making me weary to the bone. I'm embarrassed to say I sent Jilly off to do useless errands so I could be alone in my home for a moment.

The meeting with First Woman shaped the rest of my life. I became an artist so I could capture her in oil or watercolor. I took up photography to chase her shadow on film. I wrote to feel her hand cover mine over the pen. I married my wife because she reminded me of First Woman. She was a good wife to me, too, and soon, I will find her again.

I think it is time for a rest. I am an old man. After the last session I crabbed back into my room and stretched out on the bed for nearly an hour until Jilly returned and came back to see that I was all right. I didn't tell her that it is only there, in my dreams, that I see First Woman. She is always there, whenever I seek her guidance. Refreshed from my nap, I told Jilly that we would do one more session after lunch. It is time to finish this story now.

Day Four

Afternoon Recording Session

"Are you ready, my dear?"

"Yes, Grandpa."

After First Woman told me a small part of her story, she became very no-nonsense and marched through the instructions efficiently. She went back into the gray walled structure and came back holding a nested set of metal bowls. They were of a deep, bronze color with thin rims of colored enamel, four bowls in all.

"Pretty, aren't they?" She picked each one up and set them side by side on the slab of cottonwood. With a tiny cloth-ended mallet, she tapped each one and a beautiful sound rang out. "I am using these to illustrate this lesson for you. I told you earlier that this chamber of open potential in the brains of The Weavers was fragile, a container only that must be filled. Actually, the inner chamber of the brain depends upon this nest of containers. This first, the smallest, is the mother and her womb. This next size is father and family. The third is the community, meaning everything from a neighborhood to the larger human community. The fourth bowl is the natural world and its many attending realms and worlds." As she spoke of each bowl, she tapped its edge and when all four bowls were singing together, that single fine sound seemed to contain all the music and stories of all the people perfectly harmonized into one sound. "Do you hear it?"

I was transfixed by that rare sound and could only nod.

First Woman touched a fingertip on each bowl to still the sound. She laughed. "That sound will put you into meditation and prayer. In fact, that sound *is* mediation and prayer."

She rapped each edge again with the mallet and let the sound sing out across the turquoise pool. I listened, feeling strangely moved and emotional. I never wanted it to stop ringing. This time she let the sound die out naturally, but even after the ringing had stopped, I could still hear it in my ears.

"They are nested, Albert. This is so important to remember. Each container holds the next container." She reached a hand toward the ground and a pretty silver pitcher was in her hand. First Woman nested the bowls together again and poured the water into the center bowl. When it was filled it poured out into the next bowl, and when that was filled, it poured out into the next, and so on until the water flowed back out onto the earth itself. "Do you see, Albert? Life, or more precisely spirit, is such an overflowing thing that if we just let it flow naturally it will fill every container. It flows from one container to the next, from one generation to the next and on and on. It is unending, this flow. But the nest of bowls must be in order. Do you see?"

"Yes, I see."

"Good. Then you see there is an order here that must be followed."

"Yes."

"Good." She pointed to the pitcher of water and put it in my hands. "This is the energy of life itself vibrating. It is creative; it fills and empties and contains us all. I have it in this pitcher but, in truth, it cannot be contained by anything and yet is contained by everything. Do you understand?"

I did understand, and nodded, feeling like a schoolboy sitting beside my pretty teacher with the pretty bowls. Later, this lesson would prove to be both the

89

simplest lesson—and the most difficult. The energy that is life, mysterious, felt and yet not felt, seen and yet not seen. It is immeasurable.

"Albert, when you understand this natural order of things, it becomes easier to be a Watcher, easier to see when a person or an institution has gone out of order. And a child in order will become a Weaver who is capable of using this special chamber in the brain in very different ways—but only with proper care and training. My instruction for training the young Weavers is quite simple really. The key is to understand that the Weavers weave; one idea into another, one thought into another, one bit of information with another, one person to another, one country to another. They are pattern makers. They do not learn by absorbing information like wads of cotton absorbing liquid but by weaving, integrating one thing with another. Our job, then, is to feed finer and finer threads and more colors onto their loom so that they can weave the vision. We could call them spider children but Weaver sounds better, don't you think? Do you understand? We do not learn—we weave."

First Woman stopped talking and gave me time to do my own weaving. I'm not sure what I had expected. I waited for more information and there was no more. She had finished the lesson with four bowls and the instruction

90

to allow the Weavers to weave. I couldn't resist asking. "That's it? That is all we need in order to enter the new time of gathering?"

First Woman shook her head. "Oh, Albert, you have no idea how difficult this simple lesson will be—for them to weave a new fabric out of the old? The challenges will be great as the Wind of a Thousand Years dies out. Earth will look like the aftermath of a great storm. The people will cling to their old identities like life rafts. They will form false camps of belonging, fearful of separating or standing alone. They will reject the Weavers in a hundred different ways, calling them names, challenging their ideas, excluding them.

Only those firmly planted in their families, whose center bowl can overflow into the other bowls, will be able to proceed. Old institutions of health and education and economy will collapse, and we must pay careful attention to the families and the food supply. The only grace is that it is the right time, and more and more will weave their connections between this earthly realm and the other realms. Help will come from other places. But the challenge will be great. Come, walk to the waterfall with me, and then you must go."

First Woman took my hand and together we followed the footpath to the edge of the twin falls. Neither of us spoke for many minutes. We walked, both lost in our own thoughts of spider children and weavers and the new world. Once she paused and said, "Albert, remember this. The strongest thread on the Weaver's loom is always love. Only love."

I knew my time in this realm was nearly completed. We were standing at the foot of the waterfall. I saw large, fat goldfish the size of my hand in the clear stone plates that held the water. Panic rose in my throat and in my middle. I didn't want to leave this place, was afraid to crawl back into that broken body in another time and place. First Woman saw my panic. "And Albert, fear is the sharpest blade that cuts the thread of the Weaver's loom. Trust is the only thing that can mend the break."

We stood a moment staring into the falling waters. "Now, it is time for you to cleanse yourself. Walk into the shallow pool beneath the falls and put your body beneath its spray."

I started to object.

"No, Albert. All will be well. You must never cling to your belonging when it is time to separate. Go now into the falls." She dropped my hand, then handed me the small set of bowls. "Hold these close to your chest while you cleanse."

The twin streams of water flowing over the ledge were no more than ten yards away but it was difficult to force my feet to walk those ten yards. I knew. I must have known. I wondered if it was possible that the tears I'd wept earlier had merged with the waters above, and I would now be showering in my own tears.

I walked into the shallow waters and plunged beneath the falls, clutching the bowls against my chest. An explosion of water crashed over my head and shoulders. In the next instant I was blinking my eyes open in the disgustingly dirty and broken body of the Albert who had slid from his horse. Oh god, it was the cruelest of all awakenings.

"Some hot tea, please, Jilly."
"Yes Grandfather."

Albert's Notes

Jilly hurried off to fix the tea while I fought my lungs for that first deep breath all over again. She was back in just minutes pressing the cup into my trembling hands and murmuring, "Drink, Grandpa. It will restore you."

I gasped. "Ah, Jilly. You have no idea how difficult it was to leave that realm and return to this one. But I couldn't stay. It wasn't yet time for me to stay there." I gulped the tea and felt its heat burn through my body. It did restore me, and I breathed more easily.

I better get back to Jilly and finish this story. She worries about me.

"Is your little machine still on?

"Yes, Grandfather."

"Good, I feel better. Where was I? Oh yes. It was like being born again but into a broken, dehydrated body. As you young people like to say, it was gross."

"Oh Grandfather."

"See, I'm fine now, my humor returns. Let me just get the poor boy home and then we will call it a night."

As far as I could tell, there were no broken bones. My slide from the horse had been caused by the blindness, the bleeding red rain in my eyes. I was, however, dehydrated, disoriented, and weak with hunger. Unconscious and unaware, I had lain beneath that grove for two full days. Had I been in full sun, I would have died. I tried to whistle for old George, but my lips were so parched and swollen I couldn't make a sound. George, I am convinced, had his own lessons and arrangements with the higher realms because just minutes after I regained consciousness he came galloping up. I think First Woman must have sent him to get me. My duffle bag was still on his back, and I used the stirrups to yank myself upright and get to the water in my pack. I don't need to tell you in detail how filthy I was. I drank half the canteen of stale water and then threw it right up again. I think it was the smell. I smelled that bad.

My mind was fogged over and my eyes were bleary—but not blind. I was relieved to be able to see, but had no immediate recall of what had happened while I was unconscious. I was just damned glad to be alive, even in this disgusting body. My recollection of getting back up on George and making my way back home is pretty sketchy but somehow I managed it. Or George did.

When I rode up to that poor old cabin, it looked like a palace. I heard my mother scream from inside the house. Soon she and my sisters flew out of the door, off the stoop and began kissing me and crying and half carrying me into the kitchen. They asked no questions, just kept kissing and crying. I stayed awake long enough to strip to the bone and scrub and scrub and scrub. If I hadn't already been a red man, I would have been after that scrubbing.

For the first days and then weeks after my return I had complete amnesia for those two days. That space in my brain was simply closed off to me. My body healed, and my mother and sisters began to relax again. They must have sensed a change in me but they asked no questions.

The only thing that felt different at first was that my anger was gone. The demon living inside my body had left. You can't imagine what a relief it was to no longer have that raw, red energy control my days and nights. I was not like one of those sinners who suddenly finds the lord. I still liked a cold beer, but I didn't need a case of it to kill the demon any longer.

Something inside of me was different, but I didn't know what or why. I figured it was because I had lucked out and cheated death. I should have been dead after my foolish drunken ride off to rescue my father.

Mother was struggling to make ends meet I took a job on a ranch near Martin and began working long, hot days fixing fence, tossing hay, and running cattle. The work felt good, maybe for the first time. It stripped my body of all the bad influences I had dumped into it for so long. I got stronger, clearer, and healthier with each passing week. I took most of my wages and handed them to my mother without saying a word. Sometimes I'd catch her staring at me as if she was wondering what had happened to change her struggling boy into a man. But still, she didn't ask, just thanked me.

I spent time with Shawna and Silvie and was shocked to see them both becoming young women. It was as if I had not seen them—really seen them—since our father died, as if I had been living in a dark fog.

In August I turned twenty-one and marked the moment not by getting blind drunk but wondering why I no longer wanted to get blind drunk. I shot a few games of pool in Vetal, had a couple of beers, and went back to the ranch.

And then I met Sarah. And I remembered.

"Jilly, I want to stop here for the night. I need to consider how much more to tell.

"Yes, Grandfather. But you know I want to hear the rest."

"I know, dear. And you will. You will.

Albert's Notes

Jilly and I barbecued a couple of steaks and baked potatoes to celebrate the end of the telling of my two-day journey. She finished her transcription an hour ago and went to bed. I am restless, staring out the window, an eye on the world like the moon above. I'm not sure how much of my life I need to put into this story. In some ways, it feels finished right now, and in other ways the experience goes on and on and will continue to go on and on even when I am gone from this place.

When I quiet my mind and sit a moment, I realize that I want to leave my reporting of the visit to the other realms as it is. A lot of interpreting and meaning-making will just drain the energy off the basic lessons I was given. It will weaken them. Better to let them stand as is and let others do their own meaning-making, their own weaving. In many decades of study, reading, tracing the world's great philosophies, I have found nothing as clear or truthful as the simple lessons taught to me over those two days. I look out at the world from these old eyes, and I see the aftermath of the storm.

The Wind of a Thousand Years has begun to die down now, but the clean-up job is a big one. At the same time, I see the opening of the new spiral of gathering and belonging, a world of individuals seeking spirit and right place, seeking true identity and roots, finding creation. They are the Weavers. Some of them, like Jilly, are coming of age now. Beneath the tattered gray blanket, a tremendous energy builds. We are remembering to remember.

Day Five

Morning Recording Session

Albert's Notes

Jilly had to awaken me this morning. In the night, a deep weariness crept into the very marrow of my old bones followed by a piercing longing to stand on the edge of a turquoise pool filled by twin waterfalls. I told Jilly, "This will be our last session." Her look of disappointment—perhaps a touch of grief—was clear to me. "But Grandfather, you have done so many important things in your life, led so many into healing. Shouldn't we record all of that?"

"No, Jilly," I told her. "Mine has only been one life and not such an important one. All I did, I did because they asked it of me. And this," I pointed to the recorder and her tidy, growing stack of pages. "This completes what they asked of me. To tell of my visit to the realm of the ancestors."

She looked as if she wanted to weep but strengthened her spine and gave me a sweet smile. "You have to at least tell me about Sarah." She pushed play-record and smiled. We mustn't leave out the

101

romance for a twenty-three year old woman. Of course, I could never leave Sarah out. She was my heart, my First Woman.

If there is one thing I have observed in this long life, it is that every human being seeks their own First Man or First Woman, their true mate. Even you, Jilly, I told her. She blushed when I said that. Very pretty.

"Our final recording session, Jilly. Shall I begin?"

"Please do, Grandfather. I want to hear about Grandmother Sarah."

Sarah was the rancher's niece, a pretty brunette, a city girl from Minneapolis. She had come to spend the autumn with her uncle on the ranch. The first time I saw her, it was one week after my twenty-first birthday. I am ashamed to say that I didn't really see her. She was a white girl, a city girl, nothing to do with me, right? She was nineteen, and an artist. Then one day I was walking past the pump house and saw her over in the shade of the rancher's house with an easel set up. She was painting. Her long, straight hair flowed down her back. Suddenly, when I looked at her, I saw the mane of her hair shimmer and sparkle. I blinked and looked again. It appeared to be changing colors from brown to gold to deep black to pale white. It was not so much the hair itself that was changing, but a thin glow of light resting on the hair.

I stood there staring at her hair and feeling oafish, lumpy, and adolescent—and that is when I remembered. I'm not even sure how a man's memory could bring forth two entire days' worth of images in mere seconds, but mine did. It was as if a motion picture formed from beginning to end in a moment. My brain handed me the memory of my two-day journey as a complete packet stored in the golden frontal chamber of my brain.

I walked over to where Sarah was and watched in stunned amazement as she put the final brush strokes on the most vivid of my memories. On her easel was the picture of a man on a hillside curled into himself and weeping, his tears flowing in thin streams into a standing grove of trees. And woven within their midst was a stand of thin, white-barked aspen trees. I couldn't speak. I just turned and walked away.

The next day I told my boss I had to go home for a day. Instead, I drove back to where I had slid off my horse in a red rain. I got out of my old truck and walked to the exact place and sat down. There was a pile of damp leaves and beneath the leaves I felt metal. It was the stack of nested bowls that First Woman had pushed into my hand just before I went into the twin falls. Cradling the bowls in my lap, I sat beneath that tree all day and all night, staring blindly across this land while my mind retraced the path of the journey of those two days. I remembered it all—or most of it.

When the sun rose at dawn, I had 'sunk it' deep within myself. The vision has never left although small details continued to drift in over time. Whenever the smaller details came, I jotted them down on whatever was handy.

Nearly a year later, on the Fourth of July, Sarah and I were married. You see, I no longer saw her as a white woman but as a Weaver. And the fabric we wove together over our lifetime, it was a beautiful thing. We had much love.

And so ends Albert's story

Albert's Notes

Jilly applauded—my audience of one. I gave her instructions on what to do with the manuscript, and all the many slips of paper, sketches, and notes I'd saved over the years. She noted my instructions and agreed to do as asked. That evening, I took her to town to celebrate with a nice supper. It felt right to end the story there, with my marriage to Sarah. I had done as I was instructed to do. No more and no less. And like the stone that First Man had me drop again, it is a little bit hard to let go of my scraps of paper and this manuscript. Once again, I stand alone—at the beginning of a new cycle.

A Final Note from Jilly

Grandfather Albert's instructions did not include me adding this note, but I am drawn to write it anyway. The days I spent recording Grandfather's story were like no other I have ever experienced. It was as if in order to record the story, he had to take himself (and me) back to the spirit world to reclaim the information. After each session, I could recall none of what he said, a strange amnesia came over me, but it was a sweet amnesia filled with a deep joy.

I'd walk out alone at night while he rested and see, really see, that the world is made up of scintillating points of light. This lasted only a little while and then it appeared solid once again as I remembered to forget. But I remembered enough to know that this realm and the realm that Grandfather visited are composed of the same stuff.

Another odd experience I had while gathering (yes, gathering) his material was the way I'd recognize complete strangers. I'd run into town to do this or that errand and felt as though I knew all the people I saw. This is not my town—I don't know any of the people—and yet I would recognize them, as if their actual names were on the tip of my tongue. That experience didn't last either but comes back to me on occasion.

All my life Grandfather has called me his *little weaver*. I never knew why until now. I thought it was just a pet name he gave me because I liked puzzles and beading, and anything that had patterns within them. Now, I know that Grandfather saw us all--the Walkers, The Watchers, The Weavers, and yes, I read his sad note about the Weepers. All of these people, too, are familiar to me.

I am back in college now, and with each course I take, I recall Grandfather's words and smile. The physicists, the seekers and spiritualists, the new philosophers and thinkers, the scientists—they all sing the same song, the song Grandfather heard in his two-day journey.

After Grandfather completed his recording and took me out to dinner, he talked a long time about how, in just the last decade, he has seen the Weaver's hands upon the loom of the world. How I love that image. He even named a few, said he knew of many couples right here in the Black Hills and Pine Ridge who have given birth to children with extra abilities. They read through time, he told me, they read each other, they see patterns and interconnectedness in all that is around them. I got very excited and wondered at my own place in the design of this new world.

I did not share his vision, it belonged only to Grandfather, and yet my close work with him during those intense few days of recording, has given me his vision like a gift. I begin to hear and see the world and its people differently. He stepped me back far enough (10,000 years) to see the larger design. Suddenly, the world is not such a dark place but sitting at the end of a spiritual winter waiting for the bursting-forth energy of spring and the opening of a new spiral.

Grandfather did not give me permission to add this endnote to his great symphony, but I feel compelled to do so. I assume it is the spirit that directs me and, if so, I am sure he will approve. Here is what I observe as I take his lessons into my heart and the bright chamber of my mind.

- o I needn't fear loss—it is only temporary.
- o The spirit of my loved ones is inhaled with every breath I take.
- o We think we fear death, but it is the fear of not being fully alive that consumes us.
- o We desire to take life fully, bring about creation and take our full power and place in the world.
- o We simultaneously desire it—and fear it because then we may have to stand alone again for a moment. This takes great strength.
- o We are in danger of becoming a Weeper when we see only what is behind, and not what is directly around us guiding us to become more.

I'll stop now. Grandfather wanted to not interpret too much and neither should I. That is for each of us to do separately. And we do not learn—we weave.

One week after Grandfather finished recording his story, he passed one night into a peaceful coma and, three days later, went home to First Man and First Woman, to his father and mother, and to Sarah.

I would have attached his obituary here—I still would like people to know his great works in the world—but I honor his request to remain anonymous. Even in the telling of his story, he would not offer his last name or his lineage because he wanted nothing to distract from the words themselves, and the story as it stands. I did as instructed by my Elder and now his words are in the hands of another.

Jilly

About Patricia Jamie Lee

Jamie Lee traveled extensively within tribal America during the nineties with her husband, Milt Lee. Together they have produced over 60 documentary radio programs on Indian people. Lee is the author of several books including *Washaka—the Bear Dreamer* and the nonfiction book *The Lonely Place, Re-Visioning Adolescence and the Rite of Passage*. *Washaka* was awarded The Ben Franklin Award for Best New Voice in Fiction and was also a finalist in the PEN USA for Children's Literature.

Jamie Lee's short stories and essays have appeared in *The South Dakota Review, Bellowing Ark Magazine, Winds of Change Magazine, The South Dakota Magazine* and others with several stories selected for anthologies including one published by McGraw-Hill Ryerson entitled *Native Voices*. Jamie grew up in northern Minnesota and she and her husband have recently moved back and are building a straw bale house.

Other Books by Patricia Jamie Lee

Fiction

Washaka—The Bear Dreamer

One Drum,
a visionary novel set in Lakota country

Nonfiction

The Lonely Place,
Re-Visioning Adolescence and the Rite of Passage,

The Genealogy of the Soul,
A Personal Guide to Family Constellation Work

See Me Beautiful,
Charting a Path to Strength and Presence

For more stories, articles and essays from Jamie, visit her
blog, *No Ordinary Life* at www.jamieleeonline.com